JOURN
THE CENTRE
THE EARTH

— Jules Verne —

JOURNEY TO THE CENTRE OF THE EARTH

Published in this edition 1997 by Peter Haddock Ltd,
Pinfold Lane, Bridlington, East Yorkshire YO16 5BT
Reprinted 1999

© 1997 This arrangement, text and illustrations,
Children's Leisure Products Limited, David Dale House,
New Lanark, Scotland

© Original text John Kennett

Illustrated by Graham Smith (Simon Girling Associates)

ISBN 0 7105 0932 4

Printed and bound in India

Contents

To the Reader

I am sure you will have seen a film, or watched a programme on TV, that has been made from some famous book. If you enjoyed the film or programme, you may have decided to read the book.

Then what happens? You get the book and, it's more than likely, you get a shock as well! You turn ten or twenty pages, and nothing seems to *happen*. Where are all the lively people and exciting incidents? When, you say, will the author get down to telling the story? In the end you will probably throw the book aside and give it up. Now, why is that?

Well, perhaps the author was writing for adults and not for children. Perhaps the book was written a long time ago, when people had more time for reading and liked nothing better than a book that would keep them entertained for weeks.

We think differently today. That's why I've taken some of these wonderful books, and retold them for you. If you enjoy them in this shorter form, then I hope that when you are older you will go back to the original books, and enjoy all the more the wonderful stories they have to tell.

About the Author

Jules Verne, born in Nantes in 1828, is still one of the world's most popular authors. He practised law for some years before he published his first adventure story in Paris in 1862. From that time he wrote almost at the rate of a novel a year until his death in 1905. It has been said that his books are dreams come true, because he described in them the wonders of modern invention—such as submarines, aeroplanes, and television—long before they became realities.

Chapter One

The Strange Parchment

Looking back to all that has happened to me since that eventful day, I am scarcely able to believe in the reality of my adventures. They were truly so wonderful that even now I am bewildered when I think of them.

My uncle was a German, having married my mother's sister, an Englishwoman. Being very much attached to his fatherless nephew, he invited me to study under him in his home in the fatherland. This home was in a large town and my uncle was a professor of philosophy, chemistry, geology, mineralogy, and many other ologies.

One day, after spending some time in the laboratory my uncle being absent at the time—I suddenly felt hungry, and was about to rouse up our old French cook, when my uncle, Professor Von Hardwigg, suddenly opened the door, and came rushing upstairs.

"Harry—Harry—Harry—"

I hurried to obey, but before I could reach his room, jumping three steps at a time, he was stamping his right foot upon the landing.

"Harry!" he cried, in a frantic tone, "are you coming up?"

Now to tell the truth, at that moment I was far more interested in the question as to what was for our dinner than in any problem of science; to me soup was more interesting than soda and an omelette more tempting than arithmetic. But my uncle was not a man to be kept waiting.

My uncle was a very learned man and a most kind relative. I was bound to him by the double ties of affection and interest. I took deep interest in all his work, and hoped some day to be almost as learned myself. It was a rare thing for me to be absent from his lectures. Like him, I preferred mineralogy to all the other sciences. My anxiety was to gain *real knowledge of the earth*. Geology and mineralogy were to us the sole objects of life, and in connection with these studies many a fair specimen of stone, chalk, or metal did we break with our hammers.

My uncle Hardwigg was once known to classify six hundred different geological specimens by their weight, hardness, fusibility, sound, taste, and smell.

He corresponded with all the great, learned and scientific men of the age. I was, therefore, in constant communication with, at all events the letters of, Sir Humphry Davy, Captain Franklin, and other great men.

But before I state the subject on which my uncle wished to confer with me, I must say a word about his personal appearance. Alas! my readers will see a very different

portrait of him at a future time, after he has gone through the fearful adventures yet to be related.

My uncle was fifty years old; tall, thin, and wiry. Large spectacles hid, to a certain extent, his vast, round and goggled eyes, while his nose was irreverently compared to a thin file. So much indeed did it resemble that useful article, that a compass was said in his presence to have made considerable N deviation.

The truth being told, however, the only article really attracted to my uncle's nose was tobacco.

Another peculiarity of his was, that he always stepped a yard at a time, clenched his fists as if he were going to hit you, and was, when in one of his peculiar humours, very far from a pleasant companion.

It is further necessary to observe that he lived in a very nice house, in that very nice street, the Königstrasse Hamburg. Though lying in the centre of a town, it was perfectly rural in its aspect—half wood, half bricks, with old-fashioned gables—one of the houses spared by the great fire of 1842.

When I say a nice house, I mean a handsome house—old, tottering, and not exactly comfortable to English notions: a house a little off the perpendicular and inclined to fall into the neighbouring canal; exactly the house for a wandering artist to depict; all the more that you could scarcely see it for ivy and a magnificent old tree which grew over the door.

My uncle was rich; his house was his own property, while he had a considerable private income. To my notion the best part of his possessions was his god-daughter, Gretchen. And the old cook, the young lady, the Professor and I were the sole inhabitants of a very large house.

I loved mineralogy, I loved geology. To me there was nothing like pebbles—and if my uncle had been in a little less of a fury, we should have been the happiest of families. To prove the excellent Hardwigg's impatience, I solemnly declare that when the flowers in the draw-ing-room pots began to grow, he rose every morning at four o'clock to make them grow quicker by pulling the leaves.

Having described my uncle, I will now give an ac-count of our interview.

He received me in his study; a perfect museum, con-taining every natural curiosity that can well be imag-ined minerals, however, predominating. Every one was familiar to me, having been catalogued by my own hand. My uncle, apparently oblivious of the fact that he had summoned me to his presence, was absorbed in a book. He was particularly fond of early editions, tall copies, and unique works.

"Wonderful!" he cried, tapping his forehead. "Won-derful—wonderful!"

It was one of those yellow-leaved volumes now rarely

found on stalls, and to me it appeared to possess but little value. My uncle, however, was in raptures.

He admired its binding, the clearness of its characters, the ease with which it opened in his hand, and repeated aloud, half-a-dozen times, that it was very, very old.

To my fancy he was making a great fuss about nothing, but it was not my place to say so. On the contrary, I professed considerable interest in the subject, and asked him what it was about.

"It is the Heims-Kringla of Snorre Tarleson," he said, "the celebrated Icelandic author of the twelfth century —it is a true and correct account of the Norwegian princes who reigned in Iceland."

My next question related to the language in which it was written. I hoped at all events it was translated into German. My uncle was indignant at the very thought, and declared he wouldn't give a penny for a translation. His delight was to have found the original work in the Icelandic tongue, which he declared to be one of the most magnificent and yet simple idioms in the world —while at the same time its grammatical combinations were the most varied known to students.

"About as easy as German?" was my insidious remark.

My uncle shrugged his shoulders.

"The letters at all events," I said, "are rather difficult to understand."

"It is a Runic manuscript, the language of the original population of Iceland, invented by Odin himself," cried my uncle, angry at my ignorance.

I was about to venture upon some misplaced joke on the subject, when a small scrap of parchment fell out of the leaves. Like a hungry man snatching at a morsel of bread the Professor seized it. It was about five inches by three and was scrawled over in the most extraordinary fashion.

This scrawl induced my uncle to undertake the most wonderful series of adventures which ever fell to the lot of human beings.

My uncle looked keenly at the document for some moments and then declared that it was Runic. The letters were similar to those in the book, but then what did they mean? This was exactly what I wanted to know.

Now as I had a strong conviction that the Runic alphabet and dialect were simply an invention to mystify poor human nature, I was delighted to find that my uncle knew as much about the matter as I did—which

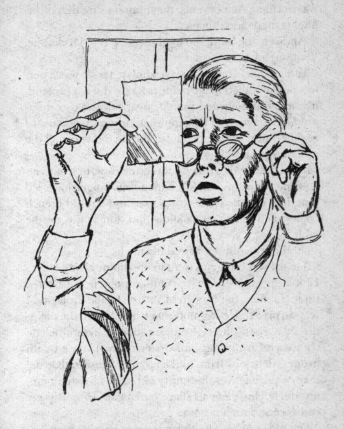

was nothing. At all events, the tremulous motion of his fingers made me think so.

"And yet," he muttered to himself, "it is old Icelandic, I am sure of it."

And my uncle ought to have known, for he was a perfect polyglot dictionary in himself. He did not pretend, like a certain learned pundit, to speak the two thousand languages and four thousand idioms made use of in different parts of the globe, but he did know all the more important ones.

It is a matter of great doubt to me now, to what violent measures my uncle's impetuosity might have led him, had not the clock struck two, and our old French cook called out to let us know that dinner was on the table.

"Bother the dinner!" cried my uncle.

But as I was hungry, I went to the dining room, where I took up my usual place. Out of politeness I waited three minutes, but no sign of my uncle, the Professor. I was surprised. He was not usually so blind to the pleasure of a good dinner—parsley soup, a ham omelette with sorrel trimmings, an oyster of veal stewed with prunes, delicious fruit, and sparkling Moselle. For the sake of poring over this musty old piece of parchment, my uncle chose not to share our meal. To satisfy my conscience, I ate for both.

The old cook and housekeeper was nearly out of her

mind. After taking so much trouble, to find her master not appear at dinner was to her a sad disappointment - which, as she watched me finish just about everything, became also alarm. What if my uncle were to come to table after all?

Suddenly, just as I had consumed the last apple and drunk the last glass of wine, a terrible voice was heard at no great distance. It was my uncle roaring for me to come to him. I made very nearly one leap of it—so loud, so fierce was his tone.

"Sit down there," barked my uncle, jabbing a long finger at the table. "I've found out one or two things."

I sat. He pushed the manuscript under my nose and laid the parchment beside it.

"They're not in the same handwriting," he said. "The parchment is much later than the book. There are letters in it that were only added to the Icelandic alphabet in the fourteenth century. It seemed to me that one of the past owners of this book most likely wrote that parchment. I know who he was because he wrote his name in the book. Look there, Axel—through this magnifying glass."

He pointed to a stain, like a blot of ink, on the back of the second page. I peered through the glass and made out the following Runic signs:

"What does it mean?" I asked.

"It's a name!" cried my uncle triumphantly. "The

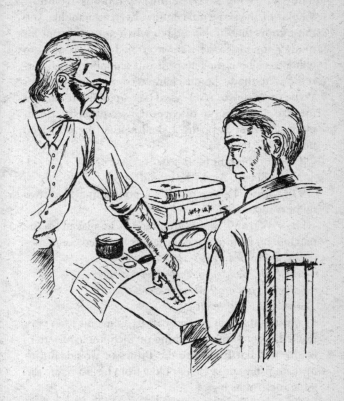

name of Arne Saknussemm—a famous Icelandic scholar of the sixteenth century. Even an idiot like you must know that in those days, when not writing in his mother tongue, a scholar wrote in Latin. Now, I am going to call out the letters of our alphabet which correspond to the Icelandic characters on the parchment. Write them down, Axel—and be careful not to make a mistake. I'm going to discover the secret of this document whatever happens. I shall neither eat nor sleep until I have done so."

"Oho!" I thought to myself.

"Nor will you, Axel," he added.

"Oh, dear," I thought, "it's a good thing I ate two dinners today!"

The Professor's fingers trembled as he picked up the parchment. I wrote down the letters he called out to me:

mmessunkaSenrA.icefdoK.segnittamurtn
ecertserrette, rotairsaduu,ednecsedsadne
lacartniiiluJsuratracSarbmutabiledmek
meretarsciluoYsleffenSnI

I must admit that when I came to the end I felt very excited. I could make nothing of the jumble of letters before me, but I felt sure the Professor would. But to my astonishment, a violent blow from his fist made the table rock on its legs.

"That can't be it!" exclaimed my uncle. "It's not Latin! It doesn't make sense!"

With that, he flew across the study like a cannonball, went downstairs like an avalanche, rushed out into the street and disappeared as fast as his legs could carry him.

I sighed and got on with some work I had to do, sorting and labelling a collection of minerals that had just come to us. Even so, I could not get this business of the old parchment out of my head. As soon as I had finished my job, I picked up the paper on which were the letters I had written down.

"What can they mean?" I murmured to myself.

I thought for a long time and found no answer. My brain got heated, and the letters began to dance before my eyes. Without thinking, I started to fan myself with the paper. Picture my surprise when, in one of these movements, as the back was turning towards me, I made out two Latin words, *craterem* and *terrestre!*

I saw the answer at once. To understand the message one had only to read backwards. I was filled with excitement, I bent over the table, placed my finger on each letter in turn, and read out the whole sentence aloud.

I was thunderstruck! What! Had some man once had the courage to do what that paper said? If so, my uncle mustn't know about it. He would want to do the same, and nothing would stop him. He would take me with him, and we should never come back alive. He must

not read the paper. The only thing to do was to destroy it!

There was a fire burning in the hearth. With a trembling hand, I picked up my sheet of paper and the parchment as well. I was about to hurl them both into the fire and destroy the dangerous secret when the study door burst open and my uncle appeared.

I only just had time to throw the wretched parchment back onto the table. My uncle paid no heed to me. Some new idea had entered his head during his walk. He threw himself into his chair and started scribbling on sheets of paper. I guessed that he was trying out the letters of the parchment in every possible order. But I knew that a mere twenty letters can have 2,432,902,800,176,640,000 different combinations! At that rate, how long might it be before I had my next meal?

Time went by; night fell; the noises in the street ceased; my uncle, bent over his task, saw nothing, not even Martha opening the door to ask: "Aren't you going to have any supper tonight, sir?"

She went away unanswered. As for me, I fell asleep on the sofa....

My uncle was still at work when I awoke next morning. His eyes were red, his face white, his hair tousled. I felt sorry for him, but still I kept my silence.

An hour or so later, when Martha wanted to leave the house to go to market, she found the front door locked.

My uncle had pocketed the key. The poor woman was much distressed, but the Professor roared at her to go away and leave him in peace.

By midday I was beginning to think that I would die of hunger. When two o'clock struck, I knew that I could keep my secret no longer. After all, perhaps my uncle would just treat it as a joke.

"Uncle Otto!" I said.

"Eh?" he mumbled, like a man suddenly roused from sleep.

"I—I know how to read the parchment. There," I said, handing him the sheet of paper on which I had written. "Read that."

"It's meaningless," he answered, beginning to crumple the paper in his hand.

"Not if you read it *backwards*—"

He opened the paper again and stared at the words upon it; then, with misty eyes and in a broken voice, he read out these words:

In Sneffels Yoculis craterem kem delibat umbra Scartaris Julii intra calendas descende, audias viator, et terrestre centrum attinges. Kod feci. Arne Saknussemm.

Which bad Latin you may take to mean:

Descend into the crater of Sneffels Yokul, over which the shadow of Scartaris falls before the kalends of July, bold traveller, and you will reach the centre of the earth. I have done this. Arne Saknussemm;

When he had finished reading, my uncle's long body gave a jump as if he had been given an electric shock. He paced up and down, his face flushed with excitement. All at once, he swung sharply upon me.

"What time is it?" he asked.

"Three o'clock," I replied.

"Is it really? My dinner has gone down quickly. I'm dying of hunger. Let's have something to eat. After that, my boy...."

"After that?"

"You can pack my box."

"What?" I exclaimed, with a feeling of dread.

"And your own," said the pitiless Professor, and went marching off to the dining room.

Chapter Two

I Argue in Vain

I stood for a moment, shuddering at the thought of what my uncle planned to do. To go to the centre of the earth! What a crazy idea! And, moreover, to expect that I would follow him there!

In the dining room I found him glaring furiously at an empty table while he roared out curses fit to curdle the blood. I told him the fault was his. He calmed down, we called Martha, and sent her running to the market. She managed so well that, an hour later, we sat down to eat a splendid meal and I felt myself grow strong again.

When we had eaten, my uncle beckoned me to follow him into his study. I did so.

"Axel," he said, "you have done me a great service; and you will share in the glory we are going to win."

"Do you really think that parchment is genuine?" I asked.

For a moment the Professor bent his shaggy brows, then he smiled and replied: "We shall see. If you have any objections to this document, speak out, my boy, don't be afraid."

"Well first of all, what do these names Yokul, Sneffels, and Scartaris mean? I've never heard them before."

"Very well—take down the third atlas in the second section of the big bookcase, series Z, fourth shelf."

I found the atlas; my uncle opened it; I bent over the map.

"As you can see in this map of Iceland, there are volcanoes all over the island." said the Professor. "You will notice that they all bear the name *Yokul*. The word means 'glacier', and is given to all the volcanic mountains in Iceland."

"I see," I replied. "But what is *Sneffels?*"

"Follow my finger along the west coast of Iceland. You see Reykjavik, the capital? Good! Now follow my finger further along this coast. What do you see there?"

"A mountain which looks as if it has grown out of the sea."

"That is Sneffels. It's five thousand feet high, and will become the most famous mountain in the world if its crater leads to the centre of the globe."

"But that's impossible!" I cried.

"Impossible!" said the Professor, in a stern voice. "Why, may I ask?"

"Because the crater must be full of lava and burning rocks, and in that case—"

"Sneffels is an extinct volcano," replied my uncle coldly. "It has had only one eruption known to history,

and that was in 1229. It is no longer counted among the active volcanoes."

"And what is this talk of *Scartaris?*"

"It would be clear enough to any but an idiot," said the Professor in an acid voice. "Sneffels has several craters. It was necessary for Arne Saknussemm to indicate the one which leads to the centre of the earth. He saw that, towards the end of June, one of the peaks of the mountain, a peak called Scartaris, cast its shadow as far as the mouth of the crater in question. When we reach the summit of Sneffels we shall know, without doubt, which way to go."

My uncle had an answer for everything, but I would not yet give in.

"All right," I said, "the old Icelander went to the top of Sneffels, he saw the shadow of Scartaris touch the edge of the crater before the kalends of July, and he had heard legends that said the crater led to the centre of the earth. But as for his having gone down there and come back alive, no! I refuse to believe it!"

"Why?" demanded the Professor with a sarcastic curl of the lip.

"Because all the theories of science prove it impossible. The temperature at the centre of the earth is said to be over two million degrees—"

"And you, Axel, are afraid of melting away? Well, let me tell you, my boy, that neither you nor anybody else

knows for certain what is going on inside the earth. If the temperature inside our globe was two million degrees, then its crust could not hold the fiery gases given off by the melted rock. It would explode like the plates of a bursting boiler."

"But everyone knows," I argued, "that the surface of the globe was once red-hot; that the outer crust cooled down first; that the centre has stayed hot."

"You are mistaken," replied my uncle. "The earth grew heated because it's crust was made up of metals like potassium and sodium, which catch fire in contact with air and water. These metals caught fire when the first rains fell. Little by little, as the waters ran into cracks in the earth's crust, they started fresh fires, together with explosions and eruptions. Hence the large number of volcanoes during the early period of the earth."

"I must say that's a clever idea!" I exclaimed, in spite of myself.

I began to be shaken by the Professor's arguments; and I was moved by the sparkle of his eyes and the enthusiasm of his voice.

"Axel," he went on, "nothing is less certain than that the earth has a hot centre. In my view, it does not—but we shall see for ourselves—"

"All right," I replied, carried away by his enthusiasm. "We shall see—that is, if it's possible to see anything down there!"

"I shall make it possible, my boy. I have that very thing in mind." He came to his feet and grasped me by the hand. "My dear Axel," he cried, clapping me hard on the shoulder with his free hand, "what a wonderful thing to devote oneself to science! But come, my boy, your box isn't packed, my papers aren't in order. We leave first thing the day after tomorrow. And remember, not a word to a soul! No one else must have the idea of reaching the centre of the earth before us!"

Chapter Three

The Summit of Sneffels

I came out of the study in a daze, swayed by my uncle's enthusiasm. It was a feeling that did not last. In an hour or two all my doubts returned. Had I been listening to the ramblings of a madman? Were we, indeed, to try to reach the centre of the globe?

"It's ridiculous!" I told myself. "I've slept badly and had a nightmare!"

That night I *did* sleep badly, and the next day *was* like a nightmare. My uncle rushed here, there, and everywhere; upstairs and downstairs; out of the house and down the street; back up the street and indoors again....

All day scientific instruments, firearms, and other apparatus kept arriving. In the afternoon I sneaked out for a walk and came back to find the Professor shouting and waving his arms about in the midst of a crowd of men who were unloading goods on the path, which was already littered with rope ladders, knotted cords, torches, flasks, grappling-irons, alpenstocks, pickaxes, and tools of every kind. Poor Martha did not know where she was.

That night my fears took hold of me again. I dreamed

I was falling all the time, hurtling into bottomless depths. I awoke at five, heavy-eyed and weary. I went down to the dining room. My uncle was eating a hearty breakfast. I could not touch a thing.

At six there was a rumble of wheels outside. A carriage had arrived to take us to the station. We were off on our fantastic adventure....

My uncle had seen to everything. All went easily and smoothly. We travelled to Copenhagen, and, from there, in a little Danish schooner, the *Valkyrie,* set sail for Reykjavik on 2nd June. The voyage passed without incident. Eleven days later we were running along the ragged, battered coast of Iceland.

When we dropped anchor off Reykjavik, my uncle dragged me to the rail and pointed out, far to the north, a high mountain with a double peak.

"Sneffels!" he cried. "Sneffels!"

When we came ashore we were greeted by the Governor himself. My uncle, who had letters of introduction, said that we had come to study the geology of the island, and would like to begin by having a look at the crater of Sneffels. The Governor was kindness itself, and insisted that we stay in his own house.

Next day, he brought to us a big, strapping fellow, with red-gold hair and beard. This calm, grave man called Hans Bjelke, was to be our guide. We had to travel more than a hundred miles overland, and would have to al-

low seven or eight days for the journey. We were to have four horses—one each for my uncle and myself, and two for our baggage. Hans would go on foot.

"A splendid fellow!" exclaimed my uncle when the guide had gone off. "He little knows what a wonderful part he is going to play in the future!"

"You mean he's coming with us too. . ."

"Yes, Axel, to the centre of the earth."

Our start was fixed for 16th June, so we had forty-eight hours to pack; instruments here, arms there, tools in this package, food in that. For arms, we had two rifles and two revolvers. Why, I don't know—since we had no need to fear savages or wild beasts, or so I supposed. My uncle, however, seemed much attached to his guns; and, also, to a large quantity of gun-cotton....

For food, we had enough meat extract and biscuits to last us six months. Gin was the only liquid we were taking, but we had some flasks and my uncle counted on finding springs from which we could fill them.

At six the next morning, we were all ready to go. We shook hands with the Governor, mounted our horses, and set off under a cloudy but settled sky.

We followed a path along the coast, and made rapid progress. The landscape was dismal and lonely. In six days we saw hardly a tree or a tuft of grass. At night, we lodged in the huts of peasants, poky little places built of earth and peat, and cold places I found them.

On Tuesday, 22nd June, at six in the evening, we came to Stapi, a village of about thirty huts at the foot of Sneffels, whose people were hunters and fishermen. Here, Hans hired three Icelanders to take the place of the horses in carrying our things; as soon as we reached the crater, however, they were to turn back and leave us there.

At this point, my uncle explained to our guide that he meant to explore the interior of the volcano as far as he could go. Hans simply nodded his head. To go there, or anywhere else, was all one to him. As for me, I still had the hope that when we reached the bottom of the crater we should find no passage at all.

The next day, 23rd June, Hans was waiting for us with his companions, all laden with provisions, tools, and instruments. We had added to our baggage a leather bottle full of water, which, with our flasks, gave us a week's supply.

Sneffels is five thousand feet high. From our starting-point we could not see its two peaks against the greyish background of the sky.

We walked in single file along the edge of a huge peat bog, then crossed a plain that looked as if it had been pelted by a rain of huge rocks.

The going became harder as the ground rose. Three hours' tiring march brought us only to the base of the mountain. There we called a halt and ate a simple break-

fast. We climbed on again, scaling the slopes of Sneffels, until at last a sort of staircase appeared. It had been formed by a torrent of stones thrown out by an eruption.

By seven in the evening we had climbed the two thousand steps of this staircase. The sea stretched away more than three thousand feet below. We had reached the foot of the cone of the crater. It was bitterly cold, and the wind was blowing hard. I was exhausted. The Professor saw that my legs were failing me and called on our guide to halt. Hans shook his head and pointed down below.

"Mistour!" he said. *"Ofvanför!"*

"What does he mean?" I asked my uncle, who spoke Danish.

"Look," replied the Professor.

I looked down in the direction of the plain. A huge column of sand, dust, and stones was rising into the air, twisting about like a waterspout. The wind was driving it against that side of Sneffels to which we were clinging. If the column were to bend towards us, we should be caught up in its eddies.

"Hastigt! Hastigt!" cried our guide.

It was clear enough that we had to follow him with all speed. He started skirting the cone of the crater. Soon the dust-storm fell upon the mountain, which trembled at the shock. The stones caught up in the wind rained

down as in an eruption. Fortunately, we were now on the opposite side and sheltered from any danger.

Hans thought it unwise to spend the night on the side of the cone. We continued our zigzag climb for five hours more. I was weak from cold and hunger, and felt I could not stand it any longer.

At last, at eleven o'clock at night, we reached the summit of Sneffels. Before taking shelter inside the crater, I had time to see the midnight sun casting its pale rays on the island sleeping at my feet.

Chapter Four
Our Real Journey Begins

We ate some supper, then settled down for the night as best we could. Next morning I awoke half-frozen by the sharp air, but in bright sunshine. I got up from my granite bed and climbed to the summit of Sneffels' southern peak. I caught my breath at the sight spread out beneath me; great cliffs hollowed out like wells, lakes reduced to ponds, and rivers turned into streams. To the west the ocean stretched as far as the eye could see.

I heard a scrape of boots, and turned as Hans and my uncle came to join me.

"Well, Axel," said my uncle, "here we are at the top of Sneffels and here are two peaks: one to the south, the other to the north. Hans will tell us the name of the one on which we are standing."

He spoke to Hans in Danish. The guide replied:

"Scartaris."

My uncle shot a triumphant glance at me.

"Now for the crater!" he said.

The crater was shaped like an upturned funnel, about a mile across at the top, and some two thousand feet deep. The bottom was not more than five hundred feet

across. It reminded me of a huge, funnel-shaped blunderbuss.

"To go down into a blunderbuss," I thought, "when it may be loaded and go off at the slightest touch!"

There was no turning back, however. It was too late for that. We snatched a quick breakfast, then Hans set off into the crater, and I followed him without a word. By noon we had arrived. I lifted my head and saw above me a round patch of sky. At one point only the peak of Scartaris stood out, rising into space.

At the bottom of the crater were three chimneys, through which Sneffels had once thrown out its stream of molten lava. Each chimney was about a hundred feet across. I was afraid to look into them, but my uncle ran from one to the other, panting for breath and muttering to himself.

Suddenly he gave a shout. He stood in the centre of the crater, his arms outstretched and his legs wide apart, in front of a huge granite rock.

"Axel!" he cried. "Come here!"

I ran over to him.

"Look!" he said.

Sharing his amazement, if not his joy, I read on the face of the block, in signs half worn away by time, this accursed name:

"Arne Saknussemm!" my uncle gloated. "Have you any doubts now?"

I made no reply, but returned gloomily to my granite seat. How long I sat there, lost in thought, I cannot say, but when I did raise my head I saw only Hans and the Professor in the crater, The three Icelanders were on their way back to Stapi. I lay down and fell into an uneasy sleep, starting up from time to time when I imagined that I could hear noises or feel tremors in the side of the mountain.

That is how our first night inside the crater went by.

Next day a grey, cloudy sky settled over the summit of the cone. This made my uncle angry, but filled me with a new hope. Of the three ways open to us, only one had been taken by Saknussemm. We should recognize it when the shadow of Scartaris touched its edge during the last days of June. If the sun did not shine, however, there could be no shadow. It was now 25th June. If the sky stayed cloudy for six more days, the expedition would have to be put off for another year!

The day wore on and no shadow appeared on the bottom of the crater. My uncle did not speak to me once. He sat, fuming and staring for hours on end into the misty depths of the sky.

Sleet fell all through the next day, and Hans built us a shelter with blocks of lava.

The next day the sky was still overcast; but on Sunday, 28th June, the sun poured its rays into the crater. Every rock, every stone, every roughness cast its shadow

on the ground. That of Scartaris stood out like a sharp edge and started turning slowly with the sun.

My uncle turned with it.

At last the shadow gently touched the edge of the centre chimney.

"It's there!" cried my uncle. "It's there! Now for the centre of the earth," he added in Danish.

I looked at Hans.

"Forut!" he said calmly.

"Forward!" my uncle echoed.

I looked at my watch. It was thirteen minutes past one. Our real journey was beginning.

I walked across to the central chimney, leaned over a rock, and looked down. Its walls dropped sheer, but were covered with countless sills and ledges which would help our descent. A rope fastened to the edge of the opening would help us on our way down, but how could we unfasten it when we arrived at the other end?

My uncle showed the way. He uncoiled a rope about as thick as a thumb and four hundred feet long. He let down half of it, then looped it over a block of lava and threw the other half down. Each of us could then descend by holding on to both halves of the rope, which would not be able to unwind. When we were two hundred feet down, we could let go of one end and pull on the other, then repeat the whole thing again.

"Right," said the Professor eagerly, "let us go down."

I heard the words with a shudder. We shared out the instruments, equipment and provisions and began our descent. Hans went over first, then my uncle, and then me. We went down in a silence broken only by the fall of loose stones. I let myself slide, clutching the double rope with one hand, and steadying myself by means of my feet and an iron-shod stick. My one fear was that the rope from which I was dangling might give way....

After half an hour we had reached a fairly wide ledge. Hans pulled one end of the rope.

The other end came down, bringing with it a rain of small stones and pieces of lava.

We looped the rope again, and half an hour later we had descended another two hundred feet. After another three hours I still could not see the bottom of the chimney.

Still we went down. We had pulled on the rope fourteen times, when suddenly Hans gave a cry:

"Halt!"

I stopped short just as I was going to hit my uncle's head with my feet.

"We have arrived," the Professor said.

"Where?" I asked, slipping down beside him.

"At the bottom of the chimney."

"Is there other way out?" I asked eagerly.

"Yes there *is* a way. I can just make out a sort of passage slanting away to the right. We'll see about that

tomorrow. Let's have our supper first, and then sleep."

We ate our meal, and settled down as best we could on a bed of stones and pieces of lava. For a while I lay in a sort of pleasant trance.

Presently after lying quietly for some minutes, I opened my eyes and looked upwards. As I did so I made out a brilliant little dot, at the extremity of this long, gigantic telescope.

It was a star with scintillating rays. After this little bit of astronomical recreation I soon fell into a deep sleep.

Chapter Four

Dead End

At eight in the morning a ray of daylight woke us up.

It was bright enough to make the rock walls sparkle, and we had no trouble in seeing around us. We made a good breakfast of biscuits and meat, washed down with a few mouthfuls of water mixed with gin.

After breakfast, my uncle consulted his instruments and made the following entries in his notebook:

> *Monday, 29th June*
> CHRONOMETER: *8.17 a.m.*
> BAROMETER: *29 inches 7 lines*
> THERMOMETER: 6°C.
> DIRECTION: E.S.E.

This last note, indicated by the compass, referred to the dark gallery my uncle had pointed out to me the previous night.

"Now," said my uncle, "our journey is really beginning."

We took up our bundles and with the Professor leading the way with a lamp we entered the gallery.

Just as I plunged into the passage, I threw back my head and caught a last glimpse of that Icelandic sky which I was never to see again.

The walls of the tunnel were lined with a shining coat of lava. The ground sloped down steeply, but we were helped by ridges that served as steps. On the roof above our heads little blisters of quartz, studded with limpid tears of glass, hung down like chandeliers and seemed to light up as we passed. Fearful as I was, I found the sight beautiful.

"It's magnificent!" I cried. ' What a sight, Uncle!"

"Ah, so you're beginning to appreciate all this, are you, Axel?" said my uncle. "Well, you'll see even finer sights, I hope. Now, quick march!"

We marched. I looked often at the compass I carried and found that the passage pointed steadily south-east.

We went on for hours without a break for food and rest. About eight in the evening my uncle called a halt, and stood the lamps on a shelf in the rock. We were in a sort of cave where there was no lack of air. We could, in fact, feel breezes, but had no idea what caused them. I was so hungry and tired that I had little care, anyway.

Hans spread out some food on a block of lava and we all ate hungrily. One thing worried me: our stock of water was already half-finished.

"We've only enough water left for five days," I said uneasily.

"Don't worry, Axel. We are sure to find an underground spring."

"When?"

"When we have got through this bed of lava. How do you imagine that springs could break through these walls?"

I did not know, so I did not answer. My uncle began putting down some figures in his notebook.

"According to my observations," he said at last, "we are ten thousand feet below sea level. What is the temperature, Axel?"

The temperature, which ought to have been 8I°C. here was barely 15°C. Which gave me cause for thought!

The next day, 30th June, at six in the morning, we began the descent again. Around midday, we caught up with Hans, who had stopped.

"Ah," exclaimed my uncle, "we have come to a parting of the ways!"

We were at the junction of two tunnels, both of them dark and narrow. Which ought we to take? My uncle pointed to the eastern tunnel, and we moved inside it.

The slope of this new gallery was very slight. Sometimes we had to walk under high arches of rock, and would then have to crawl through low and narrow tunnels. The temperature all the time stayed at a perfectly bearable level.

By six in the evening we had gone five miles south, but barely a quarter of a mile in depth. My uncle called a halt for rest. We ate without much talking, and I fell asleep at once.

We went on the next day, following the path of the lava as before. After some hours I felt sure that the tunnel was tending to rise slightly. This rise became so marked that I began to slow down.

"What's the matter, Axel?" the Professor asked impatiently.

"I'm tired out," I replied.

"What, when we've nothing to do but go down?"

"I beg your pardon, but you mean go *up*. If we keep on like this, we shall return to the surface in Iceland."

The Professor shook his head with the air of a man who does not want to believe that he has made a mistake. He signalled Hans to move on, and I hurried after them. I shuddered at the thought of losing sight of them in this maze.

At noon a change took place in the walls of the gallery. The coating of lava gave place to solid rock. We had come to the rocks of the period when the first plants and animals appeared. I had not gone a hundred yards when I found the proof of this. My feet began stirring up a dust made of the debris of plants and shells. On the walls were clear imprints of rock weed and club mosses. I picked up a shell which had belonged to an animal rather like the wood-louse; then, catching up with my uncle, I said:

"Look at this."

"Well," he said calmly, "it's a shell, that's all."

"But don't you see.... ?"

"Yes, I do see. The tunnel is rising. I may have made a mistake, but I cannot be sure of that until we reach the end of this gallery."

"You would be right to go on, Uncle except for one thing."

"And what is that?"

"A shortage of water."

"Well, Axel, we must ration ourselves."

We must, indeed, I thought grimly. Our stock of water could not last more than three days no matter how careful we were.

The whole of the next day the gallery unfolded its series of arches before us. On the Friday, after a night during which I began to feel the pangs of thirst, we set off again along the winding passages of the gallery. After ten hours' walking, the walls no longer threw back the glow of our lamps. I leaned against the wall at one point, and when I took my hand away it was quite black. We were surrounded by coal.

"A coal-mine!" I exclaimed.

"A mine without any miners," replied my uncle. "These galleries were not made by men. Anyway, it's time to eat. Let's have supper."

Hans prepared some food! I ate scarcely anything, but drained the last few drops of water from my flask. Half the guide's flask was all that remained between us. That

night I could not sleep, and counted the hours till morning.

Next day we set off again and soon came upon a vast cavern. Crossing the floor of this cave we plunged into yet another tunnel. The darkness, which was almost total twenty yards ahead, stopped us from guessing the length of the tunnel. I was beginning to think it would never come to an end when, of a sudden, a wall appeared before us. We had come to a dead end.

Chapter Six
We Find Water

We stood there for what seemed a long time, staring blankly at the wall, and saying nothing. At last my uncle shrugged his shoulders.

"At least we know where we stand," he said. "We are not on Saknussemm's road, and there's nothing we can do but turn back. Let us take a night's rest."

What else, indeed, could we do?

The next day we started back early in the morning.

Our water gave out at the end of our first day's march. After that we had nothing to drink but gin. The stuff burnt my throat and I could not even bear the sight of it. More than once I nearly fell in a dead faint, but always the others urged me on.

At last, on Tuesday 7th July, crawling on our hands and knees, we arrived at the junction of the two galleries. There I dropped and lay stretched out on the lava floor. It was ten in the morning.

Hans and my uncle tried to nibble a few pieces of biscuit. Long moans escaped from my swollen lips. I fell into a deep sleep.

I came to to find my uncle bending over me and sup-

porting my head. To my amazement he put his water-flask to my lips.

"Drink," he said gently.

I stared at him stupidly.

"Drink," he said again.

I drank. A mouthful of water slaked my burning thirst. I began to mumble my thanks.

"It's the very last of the water," my uncle told me. "I kept it carefully. I knew that as soon as you reached this fork you would drop half-dead."

"Look," I said, "there's only one thing we can do now. We must go back."

There was a long silence.

"Axel," said my uncle at last, "do you want me to give up this expedition when success is so near at hand? Listen to what I suggest. While you were lying here, I went and examined the other tunnel. It goes down towards the centre of the earth, and in a few hours it will bring us to the granite mass. There we are bound to find plenty of water. I am asking you for one more day. If, after one day, we have not found water I swear that we will return to the surface."

I was touched by the effort it must have cost my uncle to make such a promise.

"Very well," I said feebly. "We'll do as you wish. Let us be on our way."

The descent began again, this time by the new gallery.

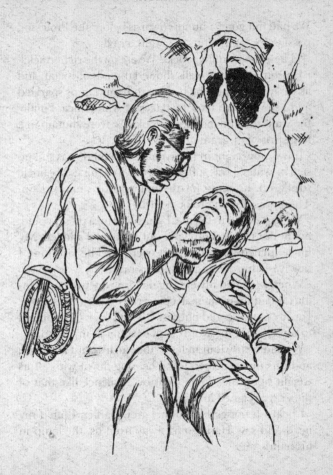

We had not gone a hundred yards before the Professor, passing his lamp along the walls, cried:

"These are primitive rocks! We are on the right track!"

For some time the walls showed threads of metal, and as we went deeper the beams from our lamps sparkled and were thrown back by flakes of white mica. Finally the walls took on a dull, sad look. We were shut up in a huge prison of granite.

It was now eight in the evening and there was still no sign of water. I was suffering agonies of thirst. My uncle strode on, listening for the murmur of some stream. There was nothing to be heard.

My legs began to fail me. I staggered on as best I could, but at last my strength gave out I groaned and fell. My uncle turned back and bent over me. The last thing I saw was a frightening gesture of rage.

When I opened my eyes again I saw my two companions rolled up in their sleeping-rugs Were they asleep? For my part, I could not rest. "It's all over," I muttered to myself, and the words kept echoing in my mind.

We had nearly four miles of the earth's crust above us, and this mass seemed to be bearing down with all its weight upon me. Time went by. A silence like that of the grave reigned around us.

I heard a noise. The tunnel grew darker. I lifted my head and saw Hans going away from us, the lamp in his hand.

Was he leaving us to our fate? I tried to shout, but my voice would not break through my parched lips. Some time later I heard the sound of footsteps again. Light flickered on the walls. Hans appeared; went up to my uncle; put a hand on his shoulder and shook him.

"*Vatten,*" said the guide. "*Vatten!*"

I had no Danish, but I understood that word. I started up. My uncle was already on his feet.

"Where is it?" he cried. "*Hvar?*"

"*Nedat,*" replied Hans.

Where? Down below. I could understand everything. Croaking and waving my arms like a madman, I lurched after Hans and my uncle down the tunnel. A half hour later we had gone a mile and a quarter, and were two thousand feet farther down. Now I could hear the sound of running water, leaping along inside the left hand wall. Hans stopped at a point where the torrent seemed closest to us. He pressed his ear against the dry stone and moved it slowly to and fro, listening intently. He was trying to find the exact spot where the noise of the water was loudest. He found it three feet up from the floor, seized his pickaxe, and began to attack the rock.

Nothing, I suppose, could be more dangerous than to take a pickaxe to this underpinning of the world. What if the wall caved in and crushed us? At that moment, however, no fear of floods could hold us back. With light and steady blows, Hans cut an opening six inches wide.

By the time the pickaxe had cut two feet into the wall, I was writhing with impatience. Then, with a loud hissing noise, a jet of water broke out of the hole. Hans was almost thrown off, balance by the shock. I heard him give a cry of pain and echoed his shout when I plunged my own hands into the jet, The spring was scalding hot.

"Let it cool," barked my uncle, holding me back.

The passage was filling with steam, while a rivulet was forming and running away down the slope. Soon we were able to take our first drink. Although the water was warm, it brought the life flowing back into our weary bodies.

"Let's fill the flasks," I said, when I had drunk my fill, "then try to stop up the opening."

"When our flasks are empty can we be sure of refilling them?" asked my uncle.

"No...."

"Then let the water run on! It must run downhill, and it will guide us as well as refresh us on our way."

"A splendid idea!" I said. "With this stream beside us, we should be able to go a long way."

The Professor laughed

"So you're feeling better already, are you, Axel?" he said. "You're coming round to my way of thinking."

"I'm not just coming round—I've come! More than that I am now confident of ultimate success. Forward!"

"I'm glad to hear it, my boy. Very well, then—a few hour's rest, and we press on towards the centre of the earth!"

I had utterly forgotten that it was night. The chronometer, however, informed me of the fact. Soon we were sufficiently restored and refreshed and had fallen into a profound sleep.

Chapter Seven

Alone

Next day we had already forgotten our sufferings.

We set off again along the tunnel with the stream running gently by our feet.

In the evening of Friday, 10th July, we worked out that we were seventy-five miles south-west of Reykjavik and seven miles down. The following morning a shaft, like the Sneffels chimney, appeared before us. My uncle crowed with joy.

"Now we shall make progress," he cried.

The ropes were fastened by Hans and we started the descent, as we had done before.

For two whole days we followed the spirals of this shaft, penetrating another five miles deeper into the earth's crust, which brought us thirteen miles below sea-level. Next day the shaft took a much gentler slope and our path became easy. Although we were a little tired, our health was good and we had not yet opened the medicine chest.

The Professor took hourly readings of the instruments—which he later published in the report on our journey. It was easy for him to pin-point our position.

We had travelled a hundred and twenty-five miles south-east of Sneffels, and now had the Atlantic Ocean over our heads. The idea no longer worried me, I found. I hardly gave a thought to sun, stars, and moon, trees, houses, and towns....

For a few days steeper slopes took us deep into the inner mass. Some days we advanced between four and five miles nearer to the centre. We kept on going, day after day after day....

By 7th August we had reached a depth of seventy-five miles, and were about five hundred miles from Iceland. That day the tunnel was but a gentle slope. I was walking in front with one lamp, my uncle was behind me with another. Suddenly, turning round, I found that I was alone.

"I've been walking too fast," I thought, "or else Hans and my uncle have stopped somewhere. I must go back and join them."

I walked back for a quarter of an hour. I saw nobody. I called out, but there was no reply. A shiver ran down my spine.

"Keep calm," I said to myself. "You'll find them again. There's only one path after all. Just keep moving back."

For half an hour I climbed the slope, listening to hear if anyone was calling me. A deep silence reigned in the long gallery. A doubt took hold of me. Had I really been in front of the others? Yes, that was certain. A thought

struck me. Fool that I was, I had a thread to guide me—
our faithful stream! I looked down. The stream was no
longer flowing at my feet.

Picture my horror and despair! I was alone and bur-
ied alive, seventy-five miles below the surface of the
earth.

Clearly, there had been some fork in the gallery. I had
taken one route, while the stream had followed another
slope and led my companions off into unknown depths.

How should I find them again? My flask was full and
I had food for three days. Should I go up or down? Up,
of course, as far as I could go. That way I was bound to
find the stream. With that at my feet, I was sure to find
my friends. There was no need for panic. I had a good
chance of reaching safety.

I went on back up the gallery, trying to recognize my
way by the shape of the tunnel. I could not even tell if
this was the way I had come. Fright took hold of me. I
broke into a run, breathing hard, shouting, staring wildly
around me. My eyes grew blurred, unseeing....

I ran headfirst into a granite wall and dropped to the
ground. The gallery had come to a dead end. I lay there
aghast. My last hope had been shattered against that
wall. More than that, my lamp had been damaged when
I fell. Its light was failing; it was going out.

There was one last flicker of light, and then I was
plunged into a thick, heavy blackness.

I was a blind man in the fullest meaning of the word.

At this point I lost my head. I stood up, my arms stretched out before me, trying to feel my way. I blundered along the tunnel, going down now, trying to run, mumbling to myself, falling and getting up again, bruising myself on the jagged rocks, all with no idea of where I meant to go. . . .

I wore myself out, of course. Finally, I pitched down in a dead faint. When my senses returned, I did not move; I simply wished that I was dead.

And then . . . I heard a sound. It was like a roll of thunder that slowly faded away in the depths of the tunnel. I took it to be some kind of underground explosion. I sat up; listened. Silence for a time, and then my ear, which was close against the wall, seemed to catch the sound of voices. I gave a start; dragged closer to the wall. Again I heard the murmur of voices. Whose? Obviously either my uncle or Hans. And if I could hear them, they could hear me.

"Help!" I shouted. "Help!"

I strained my ears for some reply from the darkness. Nothing came. A few minutes went by; again that vague murmur. I moved my ear about close to the wall until I found a place where the voices sounded most clearly. I heard my name spoken, and the voice was that of my uncle! My heart began to race. The meaning of it was suddenly plain to me. To make myself heard, I had to

speak along the wall, which would conduct the sound of my voice just as a wire carries electricity. I put my lips close to the wall, spoke as clearly as I could, and said:

"Uncle! Uncle, can you hear me?"

I waited in great anxiety. Sound does not travel quickly. Seconds, which seemed like centuries, went by, and at last these words reached me:

"Axel, is that you?"

"Yes, yes!" I replied.

"Where are you, my boy?"

"Lost, in absolute blackness."

"But your lamp?"

"It's broken."

"And the stream?"

"Disappeared."

"Take heart, my boy. Don't speak, just listen to me. I'll say it slowly. We've been up and down the gallery looking for you. Finally, we came back downstream, firing our guns. Now, you too, must come down whatever tunnel you are in. We are in a big cave, with a great many galleries leading into it. The one you are in is sure to bring you here, because all these cracks and faults seem to radiate from our cave. Get up and start walking, slide down the steep slopes, but keep coming *down*. Have you heard all this?"

"Yes...."

"Then on your way, my boy. We'll be waiting to welcome you."

These words had cheered me immensely.

"All right, Uncle," I said along the wall. "I'm leaving now."

"We'll be waiting for you, Axel. We'll be waiting. . . . "

These last words floated to me through the dark space. I set off, groping through the blackness. The slope was quite steep and I let myself slide. The speed of my descent increased. I lurched, staggered, and slithered on. I no longer had the strength to stop myself.

All at once the ground disappeared from under my feet. I felt myself falling down a long shaft, bouncing off the walls. My head struck a rock and I lost consciousness.

Chapter Eight
The Underground Sea

I opened my eyes. I was stretched out on some thick rugs. The light was dim, but I could see my uncle, bending over me. He gave a cry of joy.

"Axel, my dear boy! You're alive!" he said, and gripped my hand hard.

I became aware of Hans, looking over his shoulder.

"*Good dag,*" he said.

"Good day, Hans," I murmured. "Uncle, where are we?"

"Tomorrow, Axel, we will talk. Just now you are too weak. I have bandaged your head with compresses. Go to sleep now, and tomorrow I will tell you everything."

I was indeed very weak and let myself drop off to sleep. When I woke up next morning I stared around me in amazement. I was in a great cavern, with huge stalagmites springing up from its sandy floor. There was no torch or lamp burning, but gleams of light were filtering in through cracks in the roof. I could also hear a mysterious murmur, like the sound of waves breaking on a shore, and now and then a sound like the whistling of wind.

Had my brain been cracked in my fall, I wondered? Had my uncle brought me back to the surface of the earth? At that moment he appeared.

"Good morning, Axel," he said cheerfully. "Are you feeling better, my boy?"

"I am indeed," I replied, sitting up on the rugs.

"Hans and I took turns in watching over you. You slept well."

"I feel in fine shape—and I'm hungry."

"Oh, you shall have something to eat, my boy. Hans has rubbed your wounds with some Icelandic ointment, and they have healed wonderfully."

My uncle prepared some food, which I ate greedily. He told me that I had fallen into the cavern out of a steep shaft, and landed in the midst of a torrent of stones, bleeding and unconscious.

"Look, Uncle," I said, "I have no limbs broken—but what about my head?"

"A bump or two, but perfectly all right."

"It's not," I told him. "I must be mad, because I can see daylight, hear the wind blowing and the sea breaking on the shore. How do you explain that?"

"I can't. There is no way to do so. You'll see for yourself, and then you'll realize that geologists still have a lot to learn."

"Then let's go out," I said, starting to get up.

"No, Axel—the open air might be bad for you."

"The open air?"

"Yes, the wind is rather strong."

"I feel perfectly fit."

"Be patient, my boy. You must be strong before we begin our journey—or should I say *our voyage.*"

"Our voyage?"

"Yes . . . rest today, and tomorrow we'll set sail."

I stared at him open-mouthed. Did he mean that there was a river, a lake, or a sea outside. Was there a ship waiting for us, anchored in some underground harbour? My curiosity was stirred to fever-pitch. My uncle saw it, shrugged his shoulders, and let me get to my feet.

I was a little dizzy for a moment, then my head cleared, and I followed my uncle from the cavern.

There was a light that hurt my eyes, so that I had to cover them with my hand. When I could take it away, I stood astounded.

"The sea!" I gasped.

"Yes, " my uncle replied, " the Lidenbrock Sea. I think I have the right to call it by my name!"

Before me was a vast sheet of water that stretched away out of sight. There were waves breaking on a beach of fine golden sand, strewn with countless shells. On either hand a line of high cliffs rose up. Capes and head-lands had been eaten out of them by the teeth of the surf. It was a sea, right enough, but utterly deserted and horribly wild in appearance.

The strangest thing of all was the pale, cold light that lit a cavern big enough to contain an ocean. It was not the bright light of the sun, nor the whitish glow of the moon. The power of this light seemed, in some odd way, to be "electric".

The vault over my head, the sky if you like, was filled with huge clouds, which must at times fall in torrents of rain. As I watched, their layers opened and a ray of remarkable brightness shone down on us. But it was nothing like sunlight: there was no warmth in it. The whole scene was somehow dismal and sad. Instead of a sky shining with stars, I could feel that above the clouds was the overlapping granite, brooding and heavy upon me.

The sea might be there before me, but we were still imprisoned inside a huge cavern. I could not judge its width, since the shore stretched away on both sides as far as the eye could reach; or its length, beyond the misty backcloth of the horizon. It must have been several miles in height. The word 'cavern' cannot give any idea of this huge space. However, after being shut up in dark tunnels for more than forty days it was wonderful to breathe the moist, salty air.

"Do you feel strong enough to walk about a little?" my uncle asked me.

"Yes," I replied. "I should like nothing better."

We began to walk along the shore. Turning a head-

land, we saw, five hundred yards away, a forest. Its trees were shaped like parasols, and their foliage was unmoved by the wind.

What were they? Something unknown on the earth above? We went to see. As we drew close, my uncle called them by their name.

"It's a forest of mushrooms," he said.

He was right. They were white mushrooms, on a gigantic scale, forty feet high.

We wandered on. Other trees stood here and there in groups and clusters, and I saw that they were the lowly shrubs of the earth grown to great size: club moss a hundred feet high, and tree-ferns as tall as pines.

"Astonishing, magnificent, splendid!" exclaimed my uncle. "Here are our humble garden plants which were trees in the early stages of the earth! And look, Axel—at those bones!"

Scattered about the shore were gigantic bones, which looked like dried-up tree-trunks. We went close and examined them. Our excitement grew.

"Why, they're—they're the bones of prehistoric animals," I said excitedly. "Here's the lower jaw of a mastodon. And this must be the thigh-bone of a megatherium, the biggest of all those monsters. I can even see some whole skeletons. Uncle, these animals must once have lived on the shores of this underground sea—"

I broke off. I had been struck by an alarming thought. I looked around me fearfully.

"How do we know," I asked, "that they are still not roaming about in this—this lost world?"

My uncle was silent for a moment, and his eyes, too, moved all round that desolate shore.

"We don't know, Axel," he said quietly. "It seems unlikely, but—well, we just don't know. "

We turned and walked back along the shore.

The wind had died suddenly. A deep silence had fallen. I tried to see through the mists in the distance. Where did the sea lead? Could we hope to reach its far shore?

The Professor seemed to have no doubt that we could, but I was torn between hope and fear.

"Do you see, Axel," said my uncle, pointing, "the tide is rising."

"The tide!" I exclaimed.

"Yes, of course. The influence of the sun and moon can still be felt down here."

He was right, as usual. I could see that the waves were gradually moving up the shore.

"Judging by the ridges of foam," my uncle went on, "I estimate that the sea will rise about ten feet."

"Is it possible there are fish in these waters?" I asked.

"We've not seen any yet."

"Well, let's make some lines and hooks and see if we can catch anything."

"We'll try—we must find out all we can about these newly-discovered regions."

"Where are we? Your instruments must have given you some answer."

"Horizontally, eight hundred and seventy-five miles south-east of Iceland."

"And how deep?"

"I would say roughly eighty-eight miles. By my reckoning, the mountainous part of Scotland is above us. It's rather a heavy weight to carry, but the ceiling is very solid."

"And how wide do you suppose this sea to be?"

"Between seventy and a hundred miles. We shall set sail tomorrow."

"What about a boat?"

"It won't be a boat, my boy, but a good solid raft. Do you hear the sound of hammering? Hans is already at work. Come and see for yourself."

We found Hans working on the foreshore of a little bay. A half-finished raft was lying on the sand. It was made of beams, and the ground was strewn with planks and spars.

"Uncle," I said, "what wood is this?"

"It's pine—mineralized by the action of the sea-water—what is known as fossil wood."

"But it must be as hard as stone, and too heavy to float."

"That sometimes happens—but this is only partly fos-silized so far. Look!"

He threw a spar of wood into the sea. It disappeared from sight, then rose to the surface and bobbed up and down.

The raft was finished some hours later, and, once launched, it floated peacefully on the waters of the Lidenbrock Sea.

Chapter Nine
A Battle of Monsters

We set sail next morning.

The raft had a mast made of two staves lashed together, a yard made of a third, and a sail borrowed from our stock of rugs. There was no lack of ropes, and the vessel was well made.

All our equipment, and some fishing lines that I had made, were put on board and we set off. Hans had fitted up a rudder, and he took the tiller. The wind was blowing from the northwest by our compass, and we sailed before it at a good speed.

The north shore sank on the horizon and the land to east and west seemed to open outwards. Soon all land was lost to view, and had it not been for our foaming wake I might have thought the raft was still.

About midday masses of seaweed came in sight, floating on the surface. We skirted strands of the stuff that were three or four thousand feet long, huge serpents stretching away out of sight.

Evening came, but there was, of course, no dimming of the light in this sunless and moonless world. After supper I stretched out at the foot of the mast and fell

into a quiet sleep, disturbed only when I was called to stand my watch at the tiller.

Next day the weather was fine, with the clouds high up and fleecy. Hans threw in one of my fishing-lines, baited with a small piece of meat. For two hours he caught nothing and we had begun to think the waters uninhabited. Then there was a pull at the line. Hans drew it in and brought a struggling fish out of the water. My uncle examined it closely.

"It belongs to a family which has long been extinct on earth," he told me. "Notice these bony, enamel-like scales. And notice, also, that it cannot see—it has no eyes at all!"

The hook was baited again and thrown back. In the next few hours we caught a number of these fish. None of them had eyes. It seemed clear enough that the sea contained nothing but these sightless fossil fish. So, at least, we thought. The next day, however, we discovered our mistake....

There was still a fair wind and a fine sea, and we were making good headway. There was no land in sight. The horizon seemed far away.

My uncle took soundings several times, tying one of the heaviest pickaxes to the end of a rope which he let down to a great depth. No bottom. We had some difficulty in hauling back our weight.

When the pickaxe was back on board, Hans pointed

to some deep marks in the metal, and opened and shut his mouth several times. I stared at him, puzzled.

"Tänder," he said.

"Teeth!" said my uncle grimly.

I looked at him in amazement, then peered at the iron bar.

Yes, those were the marks of teeth imprinted on the metal. But what teeth! I could not take my eyes off this bar which had been half-gnawed away. I remembered the bones on the shore, and shuddered at the thought of those great reptiles which had once held sway over the earth. They had grown to huge size, and had great strength. No human has ever seen them alive. In the Hamburg museum I had seen the thirty-foot skeleton of one of these creatures. Was I now to find myself face to face with the thing *alive?* No, that was impossible. Yet the iron bar bore the marks of those dreadful teeth....

I gazed in terror at the sea, shuddering to think of the hideous head that might rise up above the waves. My uncle, also, was watching the ocean closely.

Nothing happened, except that the wind freshened slightly. The hours passed; evening came. Hans took over the tiller. During his watch I fell asleep.

I was awakened by a violent shock. Something had struck the raft a sharp blow. The sea all around was heaving and swelling; the raft pitching about. I rolled towards the mast and clung to it.

"What's the matter?" I shouted. "Have we run aground?"

Hans was wrestling with the tiller. My uncle was beside me, clinging to the mast with one hand, and trying to hold his telescope to his eye with the other.

"Look out there!" he shouted, and pointed with the telescope.

I stared out across the water and was struck dumb with fright. Less than a quarter of a mile away, two dark and sinister shapes had reared up out of the water. One was a gigantic, turtle-like creature; the other was an immense serpent, darting its head to and fro above the waves. Either of them could have broken the raft with one snap of its jaws.

Flight was out of the question. The reptiles came nearer and nearer and moved around the raft at high speed and in gradually narrowing circles. I picked up my rifle. But what effect could a bullet have on creatures like these?

They drew closer. I got ready to fire, but Hans motioned me to stop. The monsters passed within a hundred yards of the raft, and then hurled themselves upon each other with a fury which prevented them from seeing us.

My uncle had his telescope to his eye.

"Do you see that one with the snout of a porpoise, the head of a lizard and the teeth of a crocodile?" he

shouted. "It's the fiercest of the early reptiles the ichthyosaurus!"

"And the other?"

"The other is a serpent with a turtle's shell, the deadly enemy of the first—the plesiosaurus!"

A terrible battle was now raging only two hundred yards away. I could distinctly see the two monsters at grips with each other. I made out the bloodshot eyes of the ichthyosaurus, each as big as a man's head. Its long, tapering body measured not less than a hundred feet, and I could gauge its size when it raised its paddle-like fins above the waves. Its jaws were enormous and crammed with teeth.

The plesiosaurus, a serpent with a pear-shaped body and a short tail, had four flappers spread out like oars. Its body was covered by a hard shell, and its neck, which was long and elastic, rose thirty feet above the water.

The struggles of these two frightful creatures raised mountainous waves which almost capsized our raft. Loud hissing sounds carried to our ears. They were now so locked together that we could not tell one from the other.

We watched, terrified and spellbound, ready to open fire. For nearly an hour that dreadful fight went on until suddenly both monsters sank from sight, creating a whirlpool in the water. Several minutes passed, while we waited with bated breath. Was the struggle to end in the depths of the sea?

All at once an enormous head shot out of the water, the head of the plesiosaurus. The monster was fatally wounded. I could no longer see its huge shell, but just its long neck, rising and falling, coiling and uncoiling, lashing the waves like a gigantic whip and writhing like a worm cut in two. The water spurted all around and almost blinded us.

Soon the great reptile's death-agonies drew to an end, its movements less violent, and, after some terrible twitchings, its long form stretched out in a dead mass on the waves.

Chapter Ten

The Storm

We waited fearfully for the ichthyosaurus to lift its terrible head above the waves once more. The same thought was in all our minds. Had the monster returned to its submarine cave, or would it reappear on the surface of the sea?

We saw no more of it. The wind, which was blowing hard, helped us speed away from the scene of the battle. Slowly the tension eased out of us, and tiredness took its place. We slept in turn, leaving a look-out to keep watch. When it came to my turn, I scanned the sea with anxious eyes. Nothing moved, however. The same sea; the same weather; the same unfading light—and no glimpse of land.

The hours passed and we moved into the next day. My uncle was in a bad temper. He kept sweeping the horizon with his telescope, and then folding his arms with a look of annoyance.

Another day dragged by; and then another.

By then, my uncle was in an absolute fury at seeing the ocean still stretching away before his eyes.

One thing had changed, however: the weather. The

air felt hot and heavy; the clouds hung low and had taken on a drab olive hue, growing darker all the time until they formed a single menacing mass.

The very air seemed charged with electricity, and my hair was standing on end as if it were close to an electrical machine. It seemed to me that if my companions touched me they would receive an electric shock.

"There's bad weather on the way," I said.

The Professor made no answer. He simply shrugged his shoulders.

There was a general silence. The wind dropped completely. The sail hung in heavy folds; the raft lay motionless on the sluggish sea.

"Let us reef the sail and take down the mast," I said.

"No!" cried my uncle. "Let the wind seize us! Let the storm carry us away! Provided I set eyes on a rocky shore, I don't care if it smashes the raft to smithereens!"

The words were hardly out of his mouth before a great wind came rushing out of the far ends of the cavern. The raft bounded forward, flinging my uncle headlong. I crawled over to him and found him clinging to a rope, apparently enjoying the sight of the storm.

Hans, at the tiller, did not budge. The mast held firm, although the sail swelled out like a bubble on the point of bursting. The raft flew along.

"The sail! the sail!" I cried, making as if to lower it.

"No!" bellowed my uncle, and waved me back.

"Nej!" repeated Hans, shaking his head, the wind whipping his long hair about his face.

I could see a heavy curtain of rain ahead. Before we reached it the clouds were torn apart and brilliant flashes of lightning mingled with the roll of thunder. My eyes were dazzled, my ears deafened. Hailstones beat upon me, and when they struck our tools or guns the metal flashed with light.

I felt sure the end was near. But this was only the beginning! I had grown used to the idea of storms that lasted an hour or two, and then were done. Things were different, it seemed, in that cavern under the earth. The storm raged for three whole days and nights, and all that time we sped before it in the fury of the wind.

We lived in a continuous din and uproar. Our ears bled, and when we moved our lips no sound could be heard.

Somehow we managed to make fast all our cargo, then hung on as best we could. For hours I lay in a kind of swoon, while the rain beat at me, the waves washed over my legs, and the lightning danced in great globes of fire which burst like bombs around us.

Suddenly a fireball appeared on the raft itself. We were paralysed with fear. The fireball, half white and half blue, and the size of a ten-inch shell, moved slowly over the raft, slowly, but spinning at high speed under the lash of the hurricane. It leapt on to the provision bag,

jumped lightly down, rebounded and touched the pow-
der canister. For a horrible moment I thought we were
going to be blown up; but no, the dazzling ball moved
away and approached Hans, who simply stared at it,
my uncle, who drew away from it, and then myself, pale
and trembling under its hot glare. It was spinning close
to my foot, which I tried to pull away in vain.

A smell of nitrous gas filled the air, entering our throats
and filling our lungs to suffocation.

Why was I unable to move my foot? Was it riveted to
the raft? Then I realized that the fireball had magnetized all the iron on board; the instruments, tools, and
guns were moving about and clinking as they collided;
the nails of my boots were clinging to an iron plate let
into the wood.

At last, with a great effort, I managed to pull my foot
away just as the ball was going to seize it and carry me
away too.

Suddenly there was a blaze of light. The ball had burst
and we were covered with tongues of fire.

Then everything went dark.

When I opened my eyes again the storm was still raging; the forks of lightning were flashing about like a
brood of serpents let loose in the sky. And then, even
between the rolls of thunder and the whining of the
wind, I heard a new noise. The sound of the sea breaking on rocks! I struggled to sit up, gasping for breath as

I leaned into the wind. I had a glimpse of black and jagged shapes, with the sea frothing and churning about them. I shouted to Hans, still at the tiller; to my uncle stretched out on the deck....

Next moment the raft struck solid rock and I felt myself flung through the air. The water closed over me and at the same time hurled me forward. My head crashed against something hard, and I saw a great light, and then there was only darkness.

Chapter Eleven
An Unpleasant Shock

I came out of blackness and knew that my head was hurting. I groaned and opened my eyes. I was lying on sand, under an overhanging rock. I sat up, feeling dizzy and shaken. Through blurred eyes I made out a rocky shore, and the figures of Hans and my uncle carrying something from the sea. The rain was still falling and lightning flashed over the waves. Thunder crashed above me, but I knew that I was safe, and utterly tired, I fell back and let sleep take hold of me....

I slept for many hours. It was not until the next day that I learned what had happened when the raft was dashed against the reefs of the coast. Hans had snatched me from the waves. He had dragged me from the sea, then he and my uncle had returned to the rocks to save what they could from the wreck.

While I had slept the storm had passed. I felt sore, but rested, and glad to be alive. Hunger, the fresh air, peace and quiet after all the excitement of the past few days, all had given me a good appetite. I made an excellent breakfast off preserved meat, biscuits and tea. Hans and my uncle had rescued most of our provisions from the

wreck, and we had enough food to last us weeks. They had also managed to save the instruments and most of our tools and equipment.

During breakfast I asked the Professor where he thought we were.

"It's difficult to say exactly," he said. "During the three days of storm I was not able to keep a record of the raft's speed and direction. All the same we can make an estimate. My last checks, before the storm, showed that we had covered about six hundred and seventy-five miles of sea, and were over one thousand five hundred miles from Iceland.

"Yes," I said, "so if we count four days of storm, during which our speed cannot have been less than two hundred miles every twenty-four hours—"

"That would make eight hundred miles to be added," my uncle finished for me. "That means we are two thousand two hundred and fifty miles from Reykjavik."

"So now we have the Mediterranean over our heads?"

"Well, we can't say for sure, unless we are certain that our direction has not changed. We can easily find out by consulting the compass. Let's see what it says."

He took the compass and examined the needle. After a few swings it took up a fixed position. My uncle stared, rubbed his eyes, and looked again.

"What's the matter?" I asked.

He motioned me to examine the instrument. I gave

an exclamation of surprise. The north tip of the needle was pointing to what we supposed to be the south.

I shook the compass; examined it carefully. It was in perfect condition. In whatever position I placed it, the needle stubbornly returned to this unexpected direction.

There seemed to be no doubt that during the storm a sudden change of wind had taken place and brought the raft back to the very shore from which we had started.

Picture my uncle's face! In three quick stages it showed disbelief, amazement, and finally anger. I have never seen a man so startled at first, and so furious afterwards. The fatigues of our voyage, the dangers we had undergone, all had to be repeated.

"So! Fate is having fun with me, is it?" he cried. "Well, I won't give in! We shall sail again tomorrow!"

I said nothing. It was useless to argue. There was nothing to be done but press on.

"Since I have been driven on to this part of the coast," my uncle went on, "I won't leave it until I have seen all there is to see."

"Very well," I said, "let's start exploring."

Leaving Hans to repair the raft, we set off. A mile or so inland, we came suddenly upon a wide, open stretch that was littered with bones. It looked like a huge cemetery, containing the entire history of animal life. My

uncle darted here and there, studying and examining, his eyes flashing behind his spectacles, his head nodding up and down. All at once he gave a cry, bent down, and seized a bare skull. He held it out for me to see.

"Axel," he said, his voice trembling with excitement, "it's—it's a human skull!"

He turned it over in his hands. I shared his excitement. This was an incredible find—but there was more to come. A few yards farther on we found the complete skeleton of what I can only call an "Early Man".

It was an absolutely recognizable human skeleton, perfectly preserved, though encrusted with earth and little sparkling shells. While I stood speechless, my uncle bent and tapped its breast-bone.

"Less than six feet tall," he mused, "and nothing of the ape about him. If you ask me how he got here, I will not dare to answer. Is it possible, Axel, that men lived here, in this underground world, under this false sky, being born and dying like their brothers of the upper world? More than that, my boy: we have seen live fishes and sea monsters; might not some human being—some native of this lost world—still be roaming these shores *alive?*"

It was a startling idea. It gave me the feeling that eyes were watching me so that I turned and looked all round me. I saw only the rocks, the open plain, and a patch of forest a long way off.

I waited while the Professor made notes and sketches in his pocket-book, and then my uncle, heedless of the risk of losing our way, led me farther and farther.

We came to the edge of a forest of giant trees; this time of palm and pine, cypress and yew, all linked together by a network of creepers. A carpet of moss covered the ground; a few streams wandered among the trees, and high ferns grew upon their banks. In all these trees, shrubs, and plants, there was no colour. Everything merged in one uniform hue, brownish and faded-looking. The leaves had no green, and the very flowers had neither colour nor perfume.

My uncle plunged boldly into this giant wood, and I followed him a little fearfully. In the broad clearings left by trees which time had felled and eaten away, were all the shrubs and young shoots dear to the browsing animals of every period. After the monsters we had seen battling in the waters of the Lidenbrock Sea, do you wonder that I feared we might stumble upon some fierce, flesh-eating creature of the land, one of the larger dinosaurs, big enough to hunt down and kill any of the creatures of our earth . . . .

We came, after half a mile, upon a considerable opening in the trees. On its edge I stopped short, holding my uncle back. I thought I had seen something move. I stood, holding my breath. My uncle made an impatient gesture, shook off my hand, and took another pace

or two forward. I followed. He came to a halt and held up his hand as a signal for me to stop. I heard him give a little gasp of amazement, and then he dropped behind a tangle of brushwood. Creeping to his side, I looked out into the clearing and felt a chill run down my spine. There, before my eyes, was not one, but a whole herd of gigantic animals, and I knew them to be mastodons, the massive elephant-like creatures of prehistoric times.

Chapter Twelve

The Explosion

It was a moment of fright and wonder. I saw the trunks of those huge elephants twisting about under the trees. These were not fossils, but living creatures. And there were we, alone in the bowels of the earth, at the mercy of these giant animals.

My uncle stared and stared again; and once more I heard him give a startled gasp. He turned, seized my arm, and pointed with a hand that shook.

"Look," he breathed.

I peered over his shoulder through a gap in the brushwood. Yes, I could see it, too—something at the side of the clearing, a shadow that moved and came forward into the light....

My heart almost stopped beating. There before us stood a human being, watching over that herd of mastodons . . . and he was over twelve feet tall. His head, which was as big as a buffalo's, was half hidden in a tangled growth of hair, and in his hand he was brandishing a whole bough of a tree.

A cold sweat broke out over my body. The man was more frightful than the beasts. We had stood still and

stupefied, but now I clutched my uncle's arm and pulled him away.

"Come on," I breathed, and he let himself be persuaded.

We crept back, like timid animals, through the brushwood, and then ran over the mossy ground under the giant trees.

We came out of the forest and still we ran and stumbled, over the bone-strewn plain until we came down to the sea-shore. And there we came to a halt, panting hard, overwhelmed by amazement and struck dumb with astonishment.

What were we to think? Was it a man we had seen? No, that was impossible! It must have been some trick of the light. What kind of men could live in these deep caverns of the globe? The very idea was insane.... So we argued as we walked back along the shore, and still the picture of that shaggy giant among the trees stayed clear and terrible in my mind.

Even yet, we had not come to the end of the wonders of that day. As we walked along the shore, my foot struck against some metal thing lying on the sand. I stooped, stared, and picked up a rusty dagger. We studied it together.

"It's not mine," I said, "and I know it isn't yours."

"Think, Axel, think!" said my uncle. "This is a sixteenth century weapon, such as gentlemen once car-

ried in their belts. Its blade is coated with a layer of rust
that must be several hundred years old. D'you see how
the blade is blunted and twisted? Somebody has been
here before us, and used that blade for a special pur-
pose."

"You mean—a man from earth?"

"Yes—and that man has carved his name somewhere
with this dagger. He wanted to show the way to the
centre of the earth. Come, my boy—let us search
around."

Greatly excited, we walked along the foot of the cliff,
peering at the rock face. We reached a point where the
beach narrowed. Between two projecting rocks we
caught sight of the entrance to a dark tunnel.

There, on a slab of granite, half eaten away by time—
the initials of the bold. adventurous traveller:

"A.S.," cried my uncle. "Arne Saknussemm! Arne
Saknussemm again! Well, Axel, will you any longer
doubt that the Icelander has travelled this road before
us?"

I shook my head. There was a new fire in my veins. I
forgot the dangers of the journey, and the perils of the
return. What another had done, I would do, too. If
Saknussemm had come back alive, why should we not
do the same?

I stepped towards the dark gallery.

"Let us see where it leads," I said.

Surprisingly, my uncle held me back. He was the one who stayed calm and patient.

"Wait, Axel," he said. "Let us go back to Hans first and bring the raft and all our equipment to this spot."

It was good sense, of course. We hurried back along the shore, talking nineteen to the dozen, and found that Hans had made the raft ready for an immediate start. We climbed aboard, hoisted sail, and set our course back along the coast.

We were able to bring the raft to within the twenty yards of the point we wanted. We left it moored to the shore, took up our packs and equipment, and walked to the mouth of the tunnel.

My uncle led the way with a lamp. The dark tunnel plunged straight into the rock. It was high enough for us to walk upright, but we had taken only a dozen or so paces when we were brought to a halt. The way was blocked by a great boulder of granite. We searched in vain to right and left, up and down, for a gap. Nothing. We had to abandon any hope of getting through.

I sat on the ground. My uncle strode up and down the passage. Hans stood by, as calm and unruffled as ever.

"What about Saknussemm?" I asked. "Was he stopped by this barrier?"

"No," my uncle replied. "This piece of rock must have been loosened after Saknussemm's return to the surface. Some upheaval caused it to fall and block the way."

"And if we don't destroy it," I said, "we are unworthy to reach the centre of the earth!"

This was *me* talking—not my uncle! The spirit of discovery had taken hold of me. I wanted nothing more than to know what lay on the other side of that granite block.

"There's only one thing for it—gun-cotton," I said.

"Gun-cotton?"

"Yes it's only a bit of rock to blast."

"Come then—to work!" cried my uncle.

We set Hans to work with a pickaxe, digging out a hole for the charge. I helped my uncle prepare a slow match made of gunpowder in a linen tube.

"We shall get through!" I said.

"We shall get through!" my uncle repeated confidently.

It was midnight before we had a charge of fifty pounds of gun-cotton packed inside the hole in the rock. The slow match wound its way along the gallery to a point just outside the entrance. One spark would be enough to set off the explosion.

"Tomorrow," said the Professor.

I had no choice but to wait another six hours.

The next day, 27th August, was a great date in our journey. Even now, when I think of all that happened, I feel my heart turn over.

By six o'clock we were up and about. I begged for the honour of lighting the fuse. Once I had done this, I was

to join my companions on the raft. We would then put out to sea to avoid the dangers of the explosion. The match, we reckoned, would burn for ten minutes before reaching the gun-cotton, giving me plenty of time to reach the raft.

We made a hasty meal, then Hans and the Professor climbed on board the raft. I went to the mouth of the tunnel, opened a lamp, and picked up the end of the fuse. The Professor was holding his chronometer in his hand.

"Right," he called. "Fire, my boy!"

I plunged the end of the match into the flame, saw it flare up, and ran back to the water's edge. I clambered on board the raft, we pushed off, and paddled some sixty feet out to sea. The Professor was watching the hand of the chronometer.

"Another five minutes," he said. "Another four . . . another three."

My pulse was beating half-seconds.

"Another two ... one .... Thirty seconds . . . ten . . . five . . . now!"

There came a great roar. The shape of the rocks suddenly changed before my eyes; they opened up like a curtain. A bottomless pit seemed to gape in the shore. The sea, became one great mountainous man turned into a single tremendous wave, lifting the raft high on its crest.

In a second the light gave way to darkness. The raft was moving, sweeping along at a great speed.

In spite of the darkness, the noise, surprise and terror, I knew what had happened.

On the far side of the rock that we had blown up, there had been a steeply descending tunnel. The explosion had caused the tunnel to open up and the sea, turning into a torrent, was pouring into it and carrying us along with it.

I gave myself up for lost.

Chapter Thirteen
Shot Out of a Volcano

An hour went by—two hours, perhaps—I cannot tell. We huddled close and held each other's hands to save ourselves being thrown from the raft. From time to time it struck hard against the tunnel walls, but these shocks grew less so that I guessed the shaft had widened. This was undoubtedly the way that Saknussemm had come; but we, in following, had brought a whole sea along with us.

By the way the air was whipping at my face, I knew that we were moving at high speed. I was surprised to see a bright light suddenly appear beside me. It lit up Hans's calm face. He had succeeded in lighting the lamp with which I had fired the fuse. Though its flame jumped and flickered, it shed a little light in the terrifying blackness.

I had been right in thinking that the gallery was a wide one. The light did not show us both sides at once. It did, however, show the water falling at a steep angle, its surface like a sheaf of liquid arrows shot with great force. From time to time the raft was caught by an eddy and spun round as it sped along.

My uncle and I gazed about us with haggard eyes, clinging to the stump of the mast, which had snapped in two when the sea had struck us so violently. Of our instruments, only the compass and the chronometer remained, but all the tools had gone and, worst of all, we had only a piece of meat and a few biscuits left to us.

Did that matter, I thought bitterly? Even if we had food enough for a year, how could we get out of this deep hole into which the torrent was sweeping us?

The hours went by; we clung to the raft; and slowly the light of the lamp grew fainter. Finally, it went out. The wick had burnt away, and we were left in darkness. We still had a torch left, but in that rush of air we could not have kept it alive.

After a long time I felt that our speed had increased. I really believe that we were no longer gliding, but falling. Then came a shock. Our fall had been arrested. A waterspout, a huge liquid column poured down on us, and I felt that I was drowning.

A few seconds and I found myself gulping in fresh air. Hans and my uncle were gripping my arms hard enough to break them, and the raft was somehow still bearing all three of us.

It came upon me that I could no longer hear the roar of rushing water. A silence had taken the place of the noise which had filled my ears for hours. At that moment I heard my uncle say:

"We are going up!"

"What do you mean?" I cried.

I stretched out my arm and touched the wall, grazing my hand. There could be no doubt of it: we were rising, fast!

"The torch!" cried the Professor.

Hans managed to light it, and its flame showed us the rocky wall beside us.

"As I thought," said my uncle, "we are in a narrow shaft, about twenty feet across. The water has reached the bottom of the descent, and is now rising to find its own level—taking us with it."

"Where to?"

"I don't know—but at this rate we shall get a long way."

"Yes—if the shaft has an outlet," I said. "If it's blocked up, we shall be crushed and suffocated!"

My uncle shrugged and said nothing more. We sat in silence while the raft continued to rise. As it did so, the temperature rose with it, until the air became so hot that the sweat poured from my face and body. Were we coming to a point where central heat occurred, and the heat reduced the rocks to a state of molten liquid? I feared as much, and said to the Professor:

"If we are neither drowned nor crushed, and if we don't starve to death, we may still manage to be burned alive."

"Axel," said my uncle, "you talk like a man with no will-power or courage."

"Then you haven't given up hope?" I said irritably.

"Certainly not!" replied the Professor in a firm voice.

"Then what do you suggest we do?"

"Eat what food we have left. It may be our last meal, but at any rate we shall feel like men again, instead of exhausted weaklings!"

We divided the food into three equal portions. My uncle ate his greedily and with a sort of feverish excitement; I ate slowly and without pleasure, in spite of my hunger; while Hans chewed quietly, and seemed as calm as ever.

The food put a little more hope in me. It was five in the morning, and I could hear dismal rumblings sounding through the rock. My uncle, torch in hand, was studying the face of the rock-wall as we rose.

"Eruptive granite," I heard him say. " We are still in the Primitive Period. But we are going up, we are going up! Who knows? We still have a chance!"

He had not given up. Meanwhile, the temperature was rising fast. We took off our jackets and waistcoats.

"Are we moving towards a furnace?" I asked.

"No," replied my uncle. "That's impossible—quite impossible!"

"All the same," I said, feeling the side of the shaft, "this wall is burning hot."

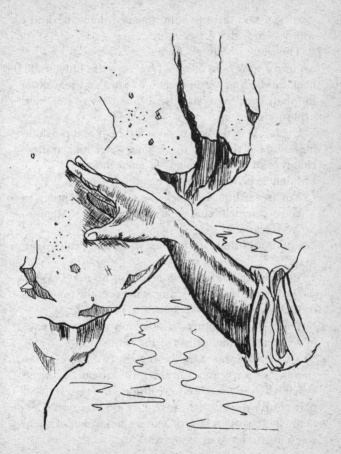

Just as I said this my hand touched the water and I withdrew it with a cry of pain.

"The water's boiling!" I cried.

A terror took hold of me. There was this unbearable heat, this boiling water, and now I saw that the walls of the shaft itself were shaking. I heard a series of loud explosions.

"Uncle," I cried, "we are done for! Look at these shaking walls, feel this heat, this boiling water, look at these clouds of steam all the signs of an earthquake!"

My uncle gently shook his head.

"Not an earthquake, Axel," he said. "An eruption."

"You—you mean that we are caught in the shaft of an active volcano?"

"I do. And I think it's the best thing that can happen to us."

The best thing! Had he gone out of his mind? What did he mean? He was peering at me over the top of his spectacles.

"Axel," he said calmly, "it's the only chance we have of returning to the surface of the earth."

I sat there, stunned by the thought. We were in the chimney of a volcano. But this time, instead of a dead volcano like Sneffels, we were inside a live one. In what part of the world, then, would we be shot out? Certainly there was no lack of craters, but which of them was going to serve us as an exit?

Still we were rising. The night went by, and toward morning we began to ascend faster and faster. Soon lurid lights began to flicker around us, and the shaft grew wider. To both right and left I noticed deep corridors like huge tunnels, from which thick clouds of steam were pouring, while crackling tongues of flame licked at the walls. There was no longer water under the raft, but a bubbling eruptive matter. The temperature had become unbearable. I had the feeling that I was melting. And then the raft came to a stop. We were no longer rising. By then I was almost suffocated, and nearly too stupid to care what happened.

The raft rose again, swiftly and jerkily, for some minutes. It stopped once more.

"This is a volcano with an intermittent eruption," my uncle shouted in my ear. "It lets us draw breath every now and then, at the same time as itself."

Suddenly we shot upwards again and had to cling to beams and lashings to avoid being flung from the raft. Again the thrust stopped....

How many times this happened I cannot say. All I know is that each time we shot up at a greater speed, and, during the brief halts, we were nearly stifled by the burning air.

I have no clear picture of what happened during the next few hours. I have a memory of continuous explosions, of shifting and shaking rocks, and a spinning

movement in which our raft was whirling around. It rocked about on waves of lava in the midst of a rain of ashes. Flames were roaring around us. Then up we went, faster than ever. I knew the terror of a man tied to the mouth of a cannon, just as the shot is fired and his limbs are scattered to the wind. The raft seemed to go hurtling into outer space. A brilliant light was hurting my eyes, and I felt myself falling, falling....

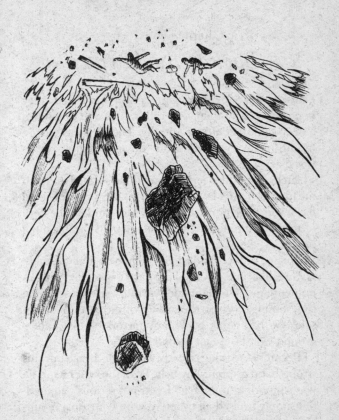

Chapter Fourteen
Back to the Surface

I struck something hard with a crash that jarred every bone in my body, then went rolling over and over down a steep slope. I could see nothing. The light was still too bright for my eyes. My head was spinning; my brain was dizzy....

I fetched up with a jerk as something seemed to clutch me from behind. I lay still, panting and gasping. I could feel a warmth on the skin of my face, and on the flesh of my body through the scorched rags of shirt that hung on me.

I opened my eyes and a fierce light beat at them, making me blink and cry. I did not care. I was filled with an immense joy. The light and warmth were those of the sun, shining down on the surface of the earth. We were safe! We had come back! The terrors of that underground world were all behind us!

I began to see things clearly. Hans was beside me, his strong hand gripping my belt. With the other hand he was supporting my uncle. I was not seriously injured, but simply bruised all over. We were lying on a mountain slope, baked by the rays of a scorching sun.

"Where are we?" asked my uncle.

His hair and eyebrows were scorched white, and he seemed to be annoyed at finding himself back on the outside of the earth.

"In Iceland," I said.

"We're certainly not there, my boy. This isn't a northern volcano. Look about you, Axel!"

Below us the land was green, plunging away into the waters of a blue sea. To the east was a little harbour, with houses scattered around it; to the west distant coasts lined the horizon, with gently curving mountains rising behind. About five hundred feet above our heads a volcano was shooting out tongues of flame, mingled with ashes and lava. I could feel the shaking of the mountain, which was breathing like a whale, puffing out fire and air through its huge blowers. Over to one side a stream of hot lava was oozing down the mountain side.

My uncle rose to his feet.

"Whatever this mountain may be," he said, "it's rather hot here. The explosions are still going on, and it would be a pity to come safely out of a volcano just to be hit on the head with a piece of rock. Let's go down and find out where we are."

The sides of the volcano were steep. We kept slipping into hollows that were filled with ash as we tried to avoid the streams of lava which were winding, hot and steaming, down the slope.

Slowly that girdle of green drew near. I was tormented by hunger and thirst, but felt it heaven to be alive and walking beneath the sun.

After two hours we came to a lovely stretch of country, covered with olive trees, pomegranates and vines. We bit off whole clusters of purple grapes, and then, not far off, we found a spring of fresh water into which we plunged our hands and faces.

As we rose to our feet, a boy stepped out from between two clumps of olive trees. He was dark of hair, skin and eye, wretchedly thin, and dressed in tatters of clothing. He saw us and stopped; then, alarmed by our matted hair and beards, our scorched and filthy rags, he turned to run. Hans was on him like a shot, however, and brought him back to us, kicking and screaming.

My uncle tried to quieten him, and asked him in German:

"What is the name of this mountain?"

The child made no reply, just stared at us out of dark and terrified eyes.

"He looks Italian to me," I said.

"*Dove noi siamo?*" said the Professor.

"Yes, where are we?" I repeated impatiently. The boy still made no reply.

"Will you answer when you're spoken to?" cried my uncle, beginning to lose his temper and shaking the child by the ears.

"Come so noma questa isola?"

"Stromboli," replied the boy, slipping out of Hans's grasp and tearing off through the trees.

We gave no thought to him. Stromboli! Oh, what a journey! What a wonderful journey! We had gone in by one volcano and come out by another more than three thousand miles from Sneffels! We had exchanged the grey fogs of the icy north for the blue skies of the Mediterranean.

We set off again in the direction of the port we had seen. It seemed to us that it would be unwise to say how we had arrived on the island. The Italians were super-stitious and would think us to be devils who had leaped straight out of hell! We would pretend to be sailors, thrown up on the island by shipwreck. This was not so glorious but far safer. On the way, I noticed that my uncle had taken our compass from his pocket and I heard him murmur:

"It pointed north! How can we explain that?"

"Good Lord," I said, "the best thing is not to explain it. That's the simplest solution."

"What! You have no scientific spirit, my boy. The idea is positively disgraceful!"

As he spoke, my uncle, half-naked, burnt, battered and bruised, with his leather moneybelt around his waist, became once more the awe-inspiring Professor of min-eralogy....

An hour later we reached the port of San Vicenzo. We were received by the Stromboli fishermen with much kindness. They gave us food and clothing, and after waiting forty-eight hours, a small craft took us on 31st August to Messina, where we rested a few days.

On Friday 4th September, we sailed on a French ship, the *Valturno*, to Marseilles, with nothing on our minds but the problem of our wretched compass, which had told us we were travelling north in those last stages of our underworld adventure. My uncle thought and pondered about little else. In the evening of 9th September we arrived at Hamburg.

Professor Lidenbrock's return caused a sensation in Hamburg. As a result of Marth's gossiping, the news of his departure for the centre of the earth had spread far and wide. People refused to believe that such a journey was possible, and when they saw him again they did not believe it any the more.

However, the sight of Hans and some pieces of news that came from Iceland helped to change their minds.

When my uncle gave our story to the press he became a great man, and I the nephew of a great man. Hamburg gave a banquet in our honour. A public meeting was held at the university, at which the Professor described all that we had done. On that same day he placed Saknussemm's parchment in the city archives, and spoke of his regret in having failed to follow in the

Icelander's footsteps to the very centre of the earth.

My uncle's fame spread all over the world. There were some, of course, who argued that he was a liar or a madman, but even they could not explain how he had vanished into the crater of one volcano and come back out of another.

While the arguments still raged we suffered a real sorrow. Hans, to whom we owed so much, went back to Iceland, home-sick for his own land. We will never forget him, and I certainly mean to see him again before I die.

There was only one thing about our journey that remained a mystery and that tortured my uncle's mind. That was the behaviour of our compass. How could it be explained? As luck would have it, I was the one who found the answer.

One day, while arranging a collection of minerals in his study, I noticed the famous compass lying in a corner and had a look at it. I gave a cry of surprise. The Professor came running into the room.

"What's the matter?" he asked.

"This compass! The needle points south instead of north! The poles are reversed!"

"Reversed?"

My uncle looked, compared the compass with another, and then gave a leap of joy which shook the whole house.

"So," he exclaimed, "when the storm drove us back

on to the shore of the Lidenbrock Sea the needle of this confounded compass pointed south instead of north. Why, why, why?"

"It's all very simple."

"Explain yourself, my boy."

"During that storm the fireball which magnetized all the iron on the raft simply reversed the poles of our compass!"

"Ah!" cried the Professor, "so it was a practical joke that electricity played on us!"

We stood there and laughed together, he the happiest of scientists because his problem was solved, and I happy to be alive on the face of the earth after all that I had seen and suffered in those dark places underground.

Illustrated Chosen Classics
Retold

Titles available in this series: